To Mum & Joe
for their inspiration
M.M.

This edition published by Parragon Books Ltd in 2013 and distributed by

Parragon Inc.
440 Park Avenue South, 13th Floor
New York, NY 10016
www.parragon.com

Published by arrangement with Gullane Children's Books
Text and Illustrations: © Mark Marshall 2007

ISBN 978-1-4723-3189-2

Printed in China

Little Lion
and the
Footprints

Mark Marshall

PaRRagon

Bath · New York · Singapore · Hong Kong · Cologne · Delhi
Melbourne · Amsterdam · Johannesburg · Shenzhen

Little Lion was playing in
the warm afternoon sun.

He especially loved to chase frogs!

But Little Lion ran too far into the jungle,
and he soon realized he was lost and alone.
He looked around and spotted some footprints.
"They could be my mom's," thought Little Lion.

And he scampered on until the
footprints led him to . . .

. . . Crocodile.

"Hello, Crocodile. Have you
seen my mom?" asked Little Lion.
"No, I haven't seen her," snapped Crocodile,
"but I will help you look."

With a splash and a mighty
flick of his tail, Crocodile was gone.
"Wait," spluttered Little Lion, "I can't swim!"

Alone again, Little Lion decided to follow a new set
of footprints. "Wow, I can fit all of my paws
in one of these!" he thought.

The enormous prints led him to . . .

. . . Elephant.

"Hello, Elephant. Have you seen my mom?" asked Little Lion.
"No, I haven't seen her," she trumpeted, "but I will help you look."

The ground shook as Elephant charged away.

"Wait for me!" panted Little Lion, but he couldn't keep up with Elephant's huge strides.

Alone again, he decided to
follow a new set of footprints.
This time they led him to . . .

. . . Monkey.

"Hello, Monkey!" called Little Lion.
"Have you seen my mom?"
"No, I haven't seen her," he
chattered, "but I will help you look."

With a loud rustle, Monkey swung though the treetops and disappeared.

"Wait, Monkey," Little Lion shouted, "I don't think I can climb this tree!"

Alone again, Little Lion wished he could find his mom's footprints.

Where can she be?

"I think it's time to go home,"
Said a familiar voice.
Little Lion spun around to see . . .

. . . Mommy!

"I've been looking everywhere for you,"
he purred, "How did you find me?"
"Well, that's simple," she said,
"I followed your footprints!"

Little Lion sat on his mom's back, and together they followed their footprints all the way home.